Scaredy Squirrel

has a birthday party

by Mélanie Watt

KIDS CAN PRESS

Scaredy Squirrel never has big birthday parties. He'd rather celebrate alone quietly up in his tree than party below and risk being taken by surprise.

Bigfoot

confetti

ponies

porcupines

So he plans a small celebration where he's the only life of the party.

BIRTHDAY PARTY CHECKLIST

A) Confirm date of birth ☑
B) Pick a safe location ☑
C) Choose party colors ☑
D) Get tuxedo dry-cleaned ☑
E) Prepare cake recipe ☑
F) Practice breathing ☑
(to blow up balloons/blow out candles)
G) Mail party invitation to myself ☐

EXHIBIT A

BIRTH CERTIFICATE

This certifies that _SCAREDY ORVILLE SQUIRREL_

was born on _OCTOBER 3RD_

at this time _1:28 AND 6 SECONDS_ in _NUT TREE_.

Weight _14.8_ grams   Height _8.24_ cm

Cute _YES_   Teeth _NO_   Fleas _NO_

Left paw print

Right paw print

OFFICIAL IMPORTANT RODENT DOCUMENT

EXHIBIT B

EXHIBIT C

Scaredy Squirrel heads down to mail his invitation. He pauses when he spots a card tucked inside his mailbox.

ROSES ARE RED,
VIOLETS ARE BLUE,
I JUST HAD TO BE
THE FIRST TO WISH A
HAPPY BIRTHDAY
TO YOU!

Sincerely,
Buddy

NAME

SCAREDY SQUIRREL

NO. (PARTY OF 1)

EXHIBIT D

221

EXHIBIT E

-NUTTY CAKE RECIPE-

2 cups flour
1 cup brown sugar
1 tsp. baking soda
1 tsp. baking powder
½ tsp. salt
1 egg
1 cup milk
¼ cup canola oil
8 cups nuts (1 cup for non-rodents)

SCAREDY SQUIRREL'S BAKING INSTRUCTIONS:
Preheat oven to 348.9 degrees and keep fire extinguisher nearby.
Verify expiration dates on all ingredients
Mix the dry ingredients then add egg, milk and oil. Do not forget the nuts! Stir clockwise.
Pour carefully into greased pan. Bake for precisely 49 minutes and 32 seconds.
Put on heavy-duty oven mitts and remove from oven.
Let cool and decorate (make it pleasing to the eye).

EXHIBIT F

SCAREDY'S BREATHING CHART

PERFECT

GOOD

OKAY

1 2 3 4 5 6 7 8 9 10 (No. of tries)

EXHIBIT G

Scaredy

YOU'RE INVITED TO SCAREDY SQUIRREL'S BIRTHDAY PARTY!

When? Today at 1:00 p.m.
Where? Nut tree, Unknown Ave.

◯ YES, I CAN
◯ NO, I CAN'T — I HAVE TO WASH MY FUR

Scaredy gives it some thought.
He decides that a kindly gesture
deserves a kindly response.

So he changes the invitation ...

Scaredy 'S BUDDY

YOU'RE INVITED TO
SCAREDY SQUIRREL'S
BIRTHDAY PARTY!

When? Today at 1:00 p.m.
Where? Nut tree, Unknown Ave.

YES, I CAN
NO, I CAN'T — I HAVE TO WASH MY FUR

But inviting a guest
is one risky move!

A few last-minute items Scaredy needs to throw a party at ground level:

safety goggles	carrot	deck of cards	earmuffs
cookies	Beethoven statue	rented party tent	fishing rod

A few surprises
Scaredy Squirrel
is afraid could
spoil the party:

clownfish

ants

DETAIL 1: SELECT CONVERSATION TOPICS FOR SMALL TALK

DETAIL 2: DETERMINE THE DOs AND DON'Ts OF PARTYING

DETAIL 3: PREPARE A BIRTHDAY PARTY SCHEDULE

1:00 p.m.	Serve punch	
1:01 p.m.	Look out for:	
1:03 p.m.	Serve dip	
1:06 p.m.	Brush teeth	
1:09 p.m.	Make small talk	
1:19 p.m.	Play a quiet game of dominos	
1:24 p.m.	Look out for:	
1:26 p.m.	Locate fire extinguisher	

1:27 p.m.	Bring out cake	
1:28 p.m.	Take a breath and blow out candle	
1:29 p.m.	Look out for:	
1:31 p.m.	Eat cake	
1:35 p.m.	Brush teeth	
1:38 p.m.	Read thank-you speech	
1:40 p.m.	Look out for:	
1:42 p.m.	Sit quietly	
2:00 p.m.	The party's over	
2:01 p.m.	Start planning next year's birthday	

Step by step, Scaredy Squirrel carefully prepares for his party. Everything is perfect, right down to the last detail.

GERM-FREE PARTY

But at 1:00 p.m. . . .

Surprise ...
Party animals
appear!

This was NOT part of the Plan!

HAPPY BIRTHDAY!

GERM-FREE PARTY

CHIPS

Scaredy Squirrel
panics!

He scatters ...

He stops the music ...

SIT!

He chases . . .

He screams . . .

He ducks . . .

He freezes and . . .

Scaredy Squirrel finally opens his eyes.

He sees that his birthday cake is lit and everyone is sitting quietly.

Scaredy blows out his birthday candle. He forgets all about the clownfish, ants, Bigfoot, confetti, ponies and porcupines.

This party is going to be a piece of cake!

HAPPY BIRTHDAY!

Afterward, Scaredy Squirrel
receives something unexpected.

FOR:
SCAREDY

A BIRTHDAY PRESENT

Inside, Scaredy finds a special surprise ...

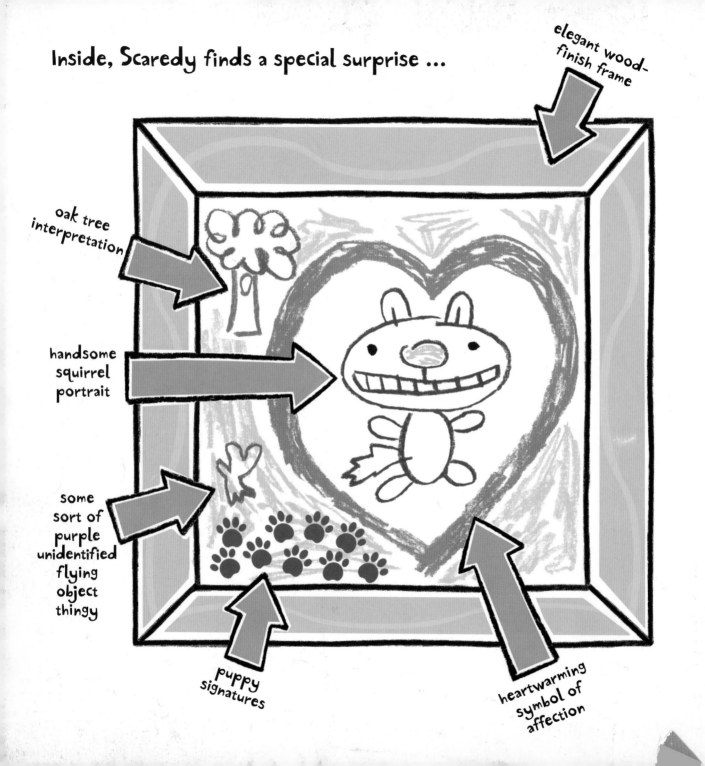

elegant wood-finish frame

oak tree interpretation

handsome squirrel portrait

some sort of purple unidentified flying object thingy

puppy signatures

heartwarming symbol of affection

Scaredy gives it some thought.
He decides that a kindly gesture
deserves a kindly response.

So he changes next year's
invitation ...

Scaredy's BUDDY Plus: Pecan,
Cashew,
Peanut,
Hazel,
Coco,
Pinenut,
Pistachio,
Mack and
Damian

YOU'RE INVITED TO
SCAREDY SQUIRREL'S
BIRTHDAY PARTY!

When? Today at 1:00 p.m. →next year
Where? Nut tree, Unknown Ave.

◯ YES, I CAN
◯ NO, I CAN'T — I HAVE TO WASH MY FUR

NEXT YEAR'S BIRTHDAY PARTY CHECKLIST

A) Confirm date of birth ☐

B) Rent larger party tent ☐

C) Choose party colors ☐

D) Dress casual ☐

E) Bake bigger cake ☐

F) Practice breathing to calm down ☐

G) Shrink-wrap everything ☐

H) Buy dog biscuits ☐

M) Put on good sneakers ☐

N) Wear top-of-the-line earplugs ☐

O) Buy toothbrushes in bulk ☐

P) Get a Frisbee ☐

Q) Install hand-sanitizer dispenser ☐

U) Rent porta-potty ☐

V) Prepare doggy bags ☐

W) Memorize the speech ☐

P.S. This birthday party left Scaredy Squirrel speechless.

thank-you speech

WARNING!

Scaredy Squirrel insists that everyone put on earmuffs before reading this book.

For Maxime, Marc-Olivier, Thomas, Cédric, Victoria, Simon, Guillaume, Camille, Jérôme, Louis, Maude and Janique

Text and illustrations © 2011 Mélanie Watt

Kids Can Press acknowledges the financial support of the Government of Ontario, through the Ontario Media Development Corporation's Ontario Book Initiative; the Ontario Arts Council; the Canada Council for the Arts; and the Government of Canada, through the BPIDP, for our publishing activity.

Published in Canada by
Kids Can Press Ltd.
25 Dockside Drive
Toronto, ON M5A 0B5

Published in the U.S. by
Kids Can Press Ltd.
2250 Military Road
Tonawanda, NY 14150

www.kidscanpress.com

The artwork in this book was rendered digitally in Photoshop.
The text is set in Potato Cut.

Edited by Tara Walker
Designed by Mélanie Watt and Karen Powers

This book is smyth sewn casebound.
Manufactured in Tseung Kwan O, NT Hong Kong, China, in 10/2010 by Paramount Printing Co. Ltd.

CM 11 0 9 8 7 6 5 4 3 2 1

LIBRARY AND ARCHIVES CANADA CATALOGUING IN PUBLICATION

Watt, Mélanie, 1975–
    Scaredy Squirrel has a birthday party / Mélanie Watt.

ISBN 978-1-55453-288-9

I. Title.

PS8645.A8845283 2011   jC813'.6   C2010-905528-4

Kids Can Press is a lorus™ Entertainment company